big
NATE
AND FRIENDS

big NATE

AND FRIENDS

by LINCOLN PEIRCE

SCHOLASTIC INC.
New York Toronto London Auckland
Sydney Mexico City New Delhi Hong Kong

ISBN 978-0-545-46801-5

Big Nate and Friends copyright © 2011 by United Feature Syndicate, Inc.
All rights reserved. Published by Scholastic Inc., 557 Broadway, New York, NY 10012,
by arrangement with Andrews McMeel Publishing, LLC, an Andrews McMeel Universal company.
SCHOLASTIC and associated logos are trademarks and/or registered trademarks of Scholastic Inc.

12 11 10   14 15 16 17/0

Printed in the U.S.A.   23

First Scholastic printing, March 2012

44

AH! THE COUNTY FAIR! THE HIGHLIGHT OF THE WHOLE SUMMER!

YOU SAID IT!

AND THIS YEAR, I'M GONNA GO ON EVERY SINGLE RIDE! I'M GONNA DO 'EM ALL!

BUT FIRST... THE **HOT DOG EATING CONTEST!**

YOU'RE SITTING NEXT TO HIM ON THE ZIPPER.

AM NOT.

NARF NARF NARF NARF

...AND SO I ONLY FINISHED **HALF** THE TEST! I COULDN'T HELP IT! MY BRAIN JUST STARTED GOING **CRAZY**!

I WAS **TRYING** TO THINK!...BUT THE NEXT THING I KNEW, I WAS MAKING UP ALL SORTS OF WEIRD LITTLE RHYMES INSIDE MY HEAD!

10/22

YOU KNOW HOW, WHEN YOU'RE TRYING TO CONCENTRATE ON SOMETHING REALLY BORING, YOUR MIND JUST STARTS TO DO SOMETHING ELSE?

98... 99... ONE HUNDRED SESAME SEEDS! 101... 102...

HEY! **HEY! FOCUS! FOCUS!**

SNAP SNAP

© 2000 by NEA, Inc.

113

123

I WONDER WHY MRS. GODFREY HATES ME SO MUCH.

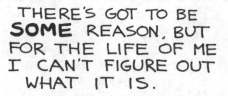

THERE'S GOT TO BE **SOME** REASON, BUT FOR THE LIFE OF ME I CAN'T FIGURE OUT WHAT IT IS.

9/25

HEY! WHY DON'T WE THINK OF ALL THE THINGS **WE** HATE ABOUT YOU, AND CROSS-REFERENCE THEM WITH STUFF **SHE** MIGHT DESPISE!

GOOD IDEA!

WELL, THERE'S HIS VOICE!

IT'S SO **NASAL!**

sigh...

146

No talking loud;
No chewing gum;
No wearing caps in school.

For every human impulse,
There is bound to be
A rule.

"No racing in
The hallways!"
Is a cry we often hear,

But who would cut
The engine
With the finish line so near?

© 2003 by NEA, Inc.

IT REALLY STEAMS ME THAT THE SCHOOL DISPLAY CASE IS DEVOTED **ENTIRELY** TO **ARTUR** AND **GINA'S** ACADEMIC AWARDS!

HOW COME IT'S ALL **THEM**? HOW COME **I'M** NOT IN THERE?

5/31

MMMF! SMIRK!

DO YOU WANT TO CONNECT THE DOTS FOR HIM, OR SHOULD I?

IT'S ALMOST CRUEL!

167

WELL, THIS IS THE FIRST ART OPENING I'VE EVER BEEN A PART OF! THE FIRST OF **MANY**, MIGHT I ADD!

I JUST WISH THEY WERE GIVING OUT **PRIZES!** I DON'T THINK THERE'S MUCH DOUBT ABOUT WHO'D GET THE BLUE RIBBON!

I MEAN, NO OFFENSE TO THE REST OF YOU, BUT I THINK IT'S CLEAR WHO'S THE MOST TALENTED ARTIST AT THIS OPENING!

SPEAKING OF OPENINGS, HOW ABOUT SHUTTING THAT BIG ONE IN THE MIDDLE OF YOUR FACE?

WHOA, TEDDY, WHOA. THAT'S THE MOUNTAIN DEW TALKING.

179

209

215